White Bird

BY CLYDE ROBERT BULLA

When John Thomas was tired of staying inside, he went out into the rain. He found that he could walk in the woods and keep almost dry. The branches were like a roof over his head.

One morning after a storm, he went to the woods. He came upon a great oak that had been struck by lightning. The trunk was split and burned. At the foot of the tree was something white.

At first he thought it was a flower or a toadstool. Then he saw it was a bird.

For Robert L. Crowell
—C.R.B.

Text copyright © 1966, 1990 by Clyde Robert Bulla. Illustrations copyright © 1990 by Donald Cook. Cover illustration copyright © 2005 by Carol Heyer. All rights reserved under International and Pan-American Copyright Conventions. Published in the United States by Random House Children's Books, a division of Random House, Inc., New York, and simultaneously in Canada by Random House of Canada Limited, Toronto. Originally published in different form by Thomas Y. Crowell Company in 1966.

www.randomhouse.com/kids

Library of Congress Cataloging-in-Publication Data
Bulla, Clyde Robert.
White bird / by Clyde Robert Bulla ; illustrated by Donald Cook.
   p.   cm. — "A Stepping Stone book."
SUMMARY: A lonely boy is found and reared by a hermit in the wilderness of the Tennessee mountains in the 1800s.
ISBN 0-679-80662-8 (pbk.) — ISBN 0-679-90662-2 (lib. bdg.)
[1. Hermits—Fiction. 2. Mountain life—Fiction.] I. Cook, Donald, ill. II. Title.
PZ7.B912Wf 1990 [Fic]—dc20 89-70231

Printed in the United States of America   27 26 25 24 23 22 21 20 19 18 17 16

White Bird

BY CLYDE ROBERT BULLA

ILLUSTRATED BY
DONALD COOK

A STEPPING STONE BOOK™

Random House 🏠 New York

Chapter 1

Luke Vail was a quiet man. He worked hard and said little. His parents had been quiet and hardworking, too. They had both died a year ago, in the spring of 1796. Now Luke lived alone in the cabin he and his father had built.

Luke had no brothers or sisters. All he had was his rocky farm in Half-Moon Valley, in the new state of Tennessee.

Luke's only neighbors were Will Barlow and his wife, Hannah. They used to watch him as he cut wood, made fences, and grew his poor crops.

"Work, work," they would say. "That's all he knows."

Then came the day that changed Luke's life.

There had been rain the night before. In the morning, he went out to look over his fields.

Part of the valley was flooded. Something was floating in the tall, green cane that grew along the river. It looked like a little boat.

Luke went toward it. It was not a boat. It was something he had not seen in many a year. It was a baby's cradle.

There was a pink quilt inside the cradle. Something moved under the quilt. Something cried in a voice like the mewing of a kitten.

He drew back the quilt. A baby looked up at him—a crying baby with a round, red face.

Luke picked up the cradle. He began to run with it, splashing water as he went. He ran all the way to the Barlows' cabin.

Hannah was in the doorway. "What on earth!" she cried.

"It's a baby," said Luke. "It's a little baby."

He carried the cradle inside. Hannah picked up the baby. "Oh, he's so cold!" she said.

Will came in. He stared at the baby, then at his wife. "What—what—" was all he could say.

"The baby was in the cradle," Luke told him. "The cradle must have come down the river."

Hannah wrapped the baby in a shirt. He put up his hands and pulled at her dress. "Poor little soul, he's hungry," she said. "Will, you take him while I warm some milk."

"I'll take him," said Luke. Very carefully he set the baby on his knee.

Will looked inside the cradle. "Here's something cut into the wood," he said. "It's two letters, *J* and *T*."

"That must be for the baby's name," said Hannah.

"Maybe *J* is for John," said Luke, "and *T* is for—I don't know. Maybe Thomas."

Hannah brought warm milk in a pan. She tried to feed the baby with a spoon.

"He doesn't know how to eat that way," said Luke.

"How else are we going to feed him?" said Hannah. "Here, baby. Here, little John Thomas. Open your mouth."

At the end of half an hour the baby was fed. He lay in his cradle and looked at the firelight on the wall.

"I wish you could talk!" said Hannah. "Then you could tell us who you are and where you came from."

"Maybe he *can* talk," said Will.

"No, he's too little," she said. "He can't be more than six months old. Poor baby. I hope your mother comes for you soon."

But weeks passed, and no one came looking for John Thomas.

By the end of summer he had grown too big for his cradle.

By winter he could walk and talk. He spent most of the time with Luke.

"It's good for Luke," said Hannah. "It gives him someone to talk to, and he does take good care of the baby."

Luke cooked cornmeal mush, and John Thomas ate it with milk and honey. In the winter, the hens laid only a few eggs, but whenever there was an egg, Luke cooked it for John Thomas.

Luke made him deerskin shoes. Hannah made him a deerskin suit.

"Such a fine boy," she said. "It's a pity he has no other child to play with."

"He won't miss what he never had," said Luke.

Chapter 2

When John Thomas was four years old, George and Jenny Barlow came to the valley.

They were cousins of Will and Hannah. One day the four Barlows came to Luke's cabin. Will and Hannah were excited.

"George and Jenny are leaving soon," said Hannah, "and we are going with them."

"We've had a hard life here," said Will. "We should have left long ago."

"There's good land waiting in the Mississippi Valley," said Cousin George. "If you have a farm there, you won't have to break your back to make a living."

"Will and I are too old to work like young people," said Hannah. "So are you, Luke. We'll all go together."

"I'm not going," said Luke.

"But you have to come with us," she said.

"This was home to my father and mother," he said. "It's home to me, too."

"We don't want to go without you," said Will.

"I told you," Luke said. "I'm not going."

"But you'll be all alone," said Hannah. "What will you do without us and John Thomas?"

"John Thomas is staying with me," said Luke.

"Oh, no!" said Hannah.

"Oh, yes," said Luke.

"What would become of him in this lonely place?" said Hannah. "He can't stay here."

"I found him. I saved him from the river," said Luke. "It's for me to say whether he goes or stays."

"Hannah," said Will. "He may be right."

"No, I won't have it!" she said. "John Thomas is going with us."

By the next evening the Barlows were ready to leave. The two wagons were loaded. The horses were tied outside the cabin. The cattle were in the pen, waiting to be driven away.

John Thomas slept in Luke's cabin that night. In the morning, before the sun was up, Luke took the boy from his bed. He dressed him and carried him outside.

John Thomas was half-asleep. "Where are we going?" he asked.

"You'll see," said Luke.

He led the boy into the woods and up a hill. They stopped behind two big rocks.

The sun came up. They could look out between the rocks and see down into the valley. They could see the Barlows' cabin and the people out in front.

One of the women went to Luke's cabin. One of the men went to the edge of the woods.

John Thomas started to go to them. Luke pulled him back. "Don't let them see you," he said.

The sun rose high. The Barlows stood in front of the cabin as if they were not sure what to do. At last they got into the wagons. The wagons began to move. Slowly they moved up the trail and out of sight beyond the hills.

John Thomas kept going to the Barlows' cabin to look for Will and Hannah.

"Are they coming back tomorrow?" he would ask.

"I don't think so," Luke would say.

After a while John Thomas stopped asking about them. He almost forgot they had ever lived there.

Every day he followed Luke.

Luke talked to him and told him stories. All the stories were from the Bible.

"Did Moses live here?" asked John Thomas.

"No, he lived across the sea," said Luke.

"What is the sea?" asked John Thomas.

"It's water. It's so much water, you wouldn't believe it," said Luke. "People sail across it in big boats."

"How big?" asked John Thomas. "As big as this house?"

"Bigger," said Luke.

"I want to ride on one," said John Thomas.

"Well, you can't," said Luke. "The sea is too far off."

As John Thomas grew older, he helped Luke more and more. He worked in the fields and garden. He carried water from the spring. He cut wood and brought it to the cabin.

"You're quick to learn things," Luke told him. "You could learn your numbers if you put your head to it."

He taught John Thomas to count. He tried to teach him to read.

They had only one book. It was a big, black Bible.

It took a long time, but John Thomas learned to read the Bible. He learned a little writing, too. He wrote with charcoal on a piece of board.

Luke said, "Now you know as much as if you'd been to school."

"Did you go to school?" asked John Thomas.

"No. My father taught me all I needed to know," said Luke. "And I can teach you all you need to know."

Chapter 3

John Thomas liked the cold winter days when he and Luke were together by the fire. Even more he liked the days when he could be outside. He went to the woods. He walked along the river.

Once he saw a raft on the river. A man and a boy were on the raft. The boy was playing with a little brown dog. He waved, and John Thomas waved back. The boy held up the dog for John Thomas to see.

"Where did you get him?" called John Thomas.

"In town," the boy called back. "I got him in town!"

"Are there any more?" asked John Thomas.

"Yes," said the boy. "There are six puppies, and—"

The raft had gone past. John Thomas could not hear the rest. He ran to the cabin to find Luke.

"I saw a raft," he said. "There was a boy on it."

"Did you say anything to him?" asked Luke.

"Yes," said John Thomas.

"Don't you ever do that again," said Luke. "The next time you see anybody, you hide in the bushes."

"Why?" asked John Thomas.

"Because strangers make trouble," said Luke.

"The boy had a dog," said John Thomas. "Luke, I want a dog. The boy said there were more, and if I—"

"That's what I mean," said Luke. "Those people didn't even stop, but still they made trouble. They made you want something you can't have."

"But if I had a dog—" said John Thomas.

"You can stop right there," said Luke. "Get on with your work. And give thanks for what you have, instead of wanting more."

John Thomas thought about the boy and his dog. In one of his dreams, he heard the boy saying, ". . . Got him in town—got him in town!"

Town was on the other side of the hills. John Thomas had never been there. He had never much wanted to go. Now, day and night, he thought about going.

At breakfast one morning he asked Luke, "Do we need anything from town?"

"Not that I know of," said Luke. "Why?"

"When you go," said John Thomas, "I'd like to go, too."

Luke gave him a sharp look. "What for?"

"To see," said John Thomas. "I'm eleven. Isn't that old enough to go to town?"

"It's no place for you," said Luke. "The world out there is full of bad people. We need things from the store sometimes or I'd never go near that hateful town."

"Did you ever see any dogs in town?" asked John Thomas.

Luke gave him another sharp look. "Are you still thinking about that dog?"

"I thought there might be one that nobody wanted," said John Thomas, "and I could—"

"Well, you can stop thinking," said Luke. "If you had a dog, you'd just get foolish over it. Then it would die or get lost, and you'd feel worse than you ever did before."

But John Thomas kept thinking about the puppies in town. All that winter he thought about the one that might belong to him. By the time spring came, he knew the puppy was grown and would never be his.

That was a strange spring. There were storms and floods. There were gray skies and cold rains.

When John Thomas was tired of staying inside, he went out into the rain. He found that he could walk in the woods and keep almost dry. The branches were like a roof over his head.

One morning after a storm, he went to the woods. He came upon a great oak tree that had been struck by lightning. The trunk was split and burned. At the foot of the tree was something white.

At first he thought it was a flower or a toadstool. Then he saw that it was a bird.

It lay very still. John Thomas wondered if it had been in the tree when the lightning struck.

He knelt by the bird, and it moved. It flopped a little way, then lay still again.

He picked it up. He could feel its heart beat. It opened one eye for a moment. The eye was pink.

The white bird was the size of a half-grown crow. It had the head and shape of a crow. But crows were black.

He took the bird home.

"What have you got there?" asked Luke. He spread out one of the bird's wings.

"What kind do you think it is?" asked John Thomas.

"It's a crow," said Luke.

"How can it be?" asked John Thomas. "It's white all over."

"Once in a while this happens," said Luke. "An animal is born all white. When I was a boy, I saw a squirrel that was white with pink eyes. But I never saw a white crow before."

"It's hurt," said John Thomas. "There's blood on its wing."

"It won't live," said Luke. "Get rid of it."

John Thomas took the bird to the woodshed and left it there.

Chapter 4

In the morning, John Thomas went to the woodshed. The bird was nowhere in sight.

He looked behind the pile of wood. There sat the bird. It gave a little squawk.

John Thomas ran back to the cabin. He asked Luke, "What do you feed a crow?"

"You don't feed it anything," said Luke. "You turn it loose."

"It can't take care of itself," said John Thomas.

He took some bread and a dish of water out to the shed. He picked up the bird. Very gently he opened its beak and fed it a bite of bread soaked in water.

"Krawk!" went the bird and opened its mouth for more.

John Thomas fed it the rest of the bread. Then the bird flopped off his knee. It hid again behind the pile of wood.

Before many days, it could eat alone. It ate from the dish and picked up the cracked corn John Thomas threw down before it.

"You've kept that ugly thing long enough," said Luke. "Turn it loose."

"It isn't well yet," said John Thomas.

"No, and it won't get well shut up in that shed," said Luke.

John Thomas wove willow branches together and made a kind of cage. He put the bird into it. "Now you won't have to stay in the dark all day," he said.

Sometimes he hung the cage in a tree. Sometimes he set it on the ground close to where he was working.

The crow was growing tame. It made clucking sounds when John Thomas came near.

One day he had set the cage down by the cabin. He was sitting on the step, talking to the bird.

"Just a little more daylight," he said, "then you have to go back to the woodshed for the night. Maybe you don't like the shed, but you're safe there. You're safe from the snakes and foxes and weasels—"

He jumped to his feet. Luke was there. Luke was saying, "I called you. Speak up when I call you!"

"I didn't hear you," said John Thomas.

"I heard *you,*" said Luke. "Talking to that bird when there's work to be done. Talking away so you can't hear when I call you."

He opened the cage door.

"Don't!" said John Thomas.

Luke had hold of the bird. He pulled it out of the cage and threw it into the air.

Half hopping, half flying, the bird disappeared into the bushes. John Thomas ran after it. He crawled into the bushes. Luke caught him by the leg and dragged him out.

"Leave it alone," he said.

"No, I've got to find it," said John Thomas.

"Leave it alone, I tell you!" said Luke. "Get on up to the spring. Get a bucket of water before dark."

John Thomas went to the spring. He brought back a bucket of water. By that time the sun was down. He knew he could not find the bird in the dark.

He hardly slept that night. As soon as daylight came, he went outside. He looked in the bushes where he had last seen the bird.

A sound came to him: "Krawk!"

He stopped. The cage was by the cabin where he had left it. And inside the cage was White Bird!

Luke came to the door. "That fool crow!" he said. "It hasn't got sense enough to fly away."

"It knows its wing isn't well yet," said John Thomas. "That's why it came back."

"What if it *never* gets well?" asked Luke.

John Thomas didn't answer, but he said to himself, "Then I'll always keep it and take care of it."

Chapter 5

Late one afternoon Luke and John Thomas finished hoeing the garden. They went to the river to wash before supper. When they started up to the cabin, they saw three strangers coming to meet them.

The strangers were two men and a boy. The men looked alike, with long faces and straggling beards. The boy was thin. His eyes were pale. His mouth hung open a little.

One of the men spoke. "I'm Len Tripp. These are my brothers, Ernie and Tad. We came to look for land to buy."

"There's none here that you'd want," said Luke.

"We found that out," said the man. "To-morrow we'll be getting on to town."

Luke said to John Thomas, "Come." They went on toward the cabin. The three brothers followed. The boy, Tad, caught up with John Thomas. "Who lives here?" he asked. "Just you and your father?"

"He's not my father," said John Thomas.

"Oh," said Tad. "Are you going to give us something to eat?"

"I don't know," said John Thomas.

Tad saw the cage in a tree beside the house. "What's that?" he asked.

"A cage," said John Thomas.

"What's in it?" Tad went closer. "It's a bird. It looks like a white crow. Is that what it is?"

"Yes," said John Thomas.

"I never saw such a thing before," said Tad. "Look at its eyes, like little red lamps. Oh, you're a pretty bird." He reached into the cage and tried to feel the bird's feathers.

"Don't hurt it," said John Thomas.

"Oh, I wouldn't hurt it," said Tad. "What's its name?"

"I call it White Bird," said John Thomas.

"That's not much of a name. I'd give it a

better one if I had it." Tad was looking into the cage. "I want this bird. Give it to me."

"No," said John Thomas.

"I'll trade you my knife for it," said Tad.

John Thomas shook his head. He took the bird out of the cage.

"What are you going to do with it?" asked Tad.

"Put it in the woodshed," said John Thomas.

"I've got a chain. It's part gold," said Tad. "I'll trade you that and the knife, too."

"No," said John Thomas. He took the bird to the woodshed.

Len Tripp was saying to Luke, "We'll be here all night. Is there room for us in your house?"

"There's more room outside," said Luke.

"You're not very friendly," said Len.

"Nobody ever said I was," said Luke.

He and John Thomas went into the cabin. The Tripp brothers were left outside.

When John Thomas woke in the morning, Luke was up and dressed.

"Where are the people?" asked John Thomas.

"Gone," said Luke.

John Thomas took corn and water out to the woodshed. The door was open. He was sure he had left it shut.

He looked inside the shed. "White Bird?" he said. He looked behind the pile of wood. The bird was gone.

"Luke!" he called.

Luke came out of the cabin.

"My bird is gone," said John Thomas. "You didn't open the door, did you?"

"No," said Luke.

"Then *he* turned it loose," said John Thomas. "That boy wanted White Bird. Maybe—maybe he *took* it!"

"He did take it," said Luke.

"How do you know?" asked John Thomas.

"I saw him," said Luke.

"You *saw* him?" said John Thomas. "You let him take it and didn't tell me?"

"Every day you had that crow with you," said Luke, "you were talking to it and making a fool of yourself. When I saw that boy take the bird, I knew it was the best thing for everybody."

John Thomas started away.

"Where are you going?" asked Luke.

"I'm going after them," said John Thomas.

"No, you're not." Luke caught John Thomas's arm.

John Thomas broke away. Again Luke caught him. John Thomas fought.

Luke dragged him to the woodshed. He pushed him inside and shut the door.

John Thomas threw himself against the door, but it was propped shut.

He sat in the dark shed thinking, "Tad took my bird. He may forget to feed it or give it water. My bird will die."

He found a log that had been cut for the fireplace. He tried to break down the door with it. The walls shook, but the door did not break.

It was nearly noon when Luke let him out.

"Do you want your breakfast?" he asked.

John Thomas shook his head.

"Then we'll get over to the field," said Luke.

They hoed weeds out of the corn. Luke watched John Thomas and kept near him. Once, John Thomas went to the spring for a drink. Luke went with him.

They worked till suppertime. They had supper. Luke lighted a candle and got out the Bible. He began to read aloud. At the end of a page he stopped. "You're not listening," he said.

"Yes, I am," said John Thomas.

"No, you're not," said Luke. "You're thinking about that bird."

John Thomas said nothing.

"That bird was no good for you," said Luke. "What I did was right. Someday you'll see."

John Thomas did not answer. He went to bed and turned his face to the wall.

Luke blew out the candle and went to bed, too, on the other side of the room.

John Thomas listened. After a long time he heard the soft sound of Luke's snoring. He slipped out of bed. He found his clothes and put them on. He felt his way to the door. It creaked when he opened it.

"John Thomas?" said Luke.

John Thomas was outside.

"Where are you?" said Luke. "Come back here!"

John Thomas was running toward the path that led up the hill. It was the path Luke took when he went to town.

Chapter 6

It was hard to keep on the path in the dark. John Thomas stopped to wait for daylight. He sat with his back against a tree, and he slept a little.

.As soon as the sky was light he went on. He took the path over the hill. He had never been so far from home before.

The path led into a wide, dusty trail. There were tracks in the dust.

Len Tripp had said, "Tomorrow we'll be getting on to town." Some of the tracks might have been made by him and his brothers.

John Thomas walked faster. He could see roofs ahead, the roofs of many houses close together.

He met a woman leading a horse. He asked her, "Are you from town?"

"Yes," she said.

"Have you seen the Tripp brothers—two men and a boy?" he asked.

"No," she said. "I don't think so."

"I'm looking for them," he said.

"Why don't you ask Dave Cressey?" she said. "He knows everybody."

"Where is he?" asked John Thomas.

"You'll see his store as you go into town," she said.

He took the trail on into town. He was between two rows of houses. Everywhere he looked, there were people. There were horses and wagons. Town was busy, and it was big. How could he ever find Dave Cressey's store?

Then he saw it. Dave Cressey's name was on a sign over a door.

He went into the store. He saw shelves and tables piled with cloth and clothing, dishes and pans. He saw barrels of flour and salt.

A man came out of the back. He was a neat-looking man in a blue-striped shirt. "What can I do for you?" he asked.

"Are you Dave Cressey?" asked John Thomas.

"That's my name," said the man.

"Do you know the Tripp brothers?" asked John Thomas.

"Let me see—" said the man.

"Two men and a boy," said John Thomas.

"Two men and a boy were in here yesterday," said Dave Cressey. "The boy had a bird."

"A white bird?" asked John Thomas.

"Yes," said Dave Cressey. "It looked like a crow, yet it was all white."

"It's mine," said John Thomas. "I have to get it back."

"You mean they stole it from you?" asked Dave Cressey.

"Yes," said John Thomas. "They came to the house in Half-Moon Valley and—"

"Half-Moon Valley?" said Dave. "Then you must be Luke Vail's boy."

"I'm not his boy," said John Thomas.

"You live with him, don't you?" asked Dave.

"I did live with him," said John Thomas. "Where did the Tripp brothers go? I have to find them."

"They took the north road out of town," said Dave. "That was yesterday. They said they were looking for land to buy. One of them said they might be back in town to-day."

"Would they be coming to your store again?" asked John Thomas.

"They might be," said Dave.

"Could I wait for them here?" asked John Thomas.

Two women came into the store. Dave told John Thomas, "Sit down. I'll talk to you in a minute."

When the women were gone, Dave said, "You've had a long walk. How about a bite to eat?"

John Thomas thought for a moment. He said, "In a store, you have to have money or something to trade, don't you? I don't have anything."

"You can pay later." Dave brought him some bread and cheese and a sour pickle. He went away while John Thomas ate.

John Thomas waited. It began to grow dark.

"They aren't coming, are they?" he said.

"It doesn't look like it," said Dave.

"I'd better go look for them," said John Thomas.

"Where would you look?" asked Dave.

"You said they went up the north road," said John Thomas.

"Yes, but it's pretty late to start out now," said Dave. "Stay here tonight, and in the morning you'd better head back to Half-Moon Valley."

"I have to find them," said John Thomas.

Dave closed the store. He brought a blanket and spread it on the floor in the back room. John Thomas slept there that night.

In the morning, he had breakfast with Dave Cressey.

"You might walk all over Tennessee and never find those Tripp brothers," said Dave. "Why don't you go back to Half-Moon Valley?"

"I have to find them," said John Thomas.

He took the north road out of town. The road became two roads. He was not sure which to take.

Back among the trees, he saw a house with a high stone chimney. He turned in at the lane that led to it.

Three dogs came rushing toward him. Their barking was fierce and ugly.

John Thomas ran. He fell into a ditch and went splashing through mud and water. He climbed out. The dogs were nearly upon him. He was under a tree. He caught a branch and pulled himself up.

The dogs ran back and forth below. They were yelping and looking up at him.

A tall black man came down the lane. A girl came running after him. She was slim and small, with light brown hair in two long braids. "Stop the dogs, Alex," she said.

The man whistled. The dogs drew back.

"What you doing up there?" shouted the man.

"That's no way to talk to him," said the girl. "After this, you'd better keep those dogs shut up."

"Yes, Miss Isabel," said the man.

The girl called to John Thomas, "Come down."

He climbed down. His clothes dripped mud and water.

"Oh, this is terrible," said the girl. "Alex, look after him."

"Yes, Miss Isabel." The man said to John Thomas, "Come along."

"But I—" began John Thomas.

"Come along," the man said again. "We all have to do what Miss Isabel says."

He led John Thomas to a shed beside the big house. He brought water and a sponge and tried to clean John Thomas's clothes.

The girl called outside, "Alex!"

Alex went to the door and came back with his arms full of clothing. He said, "You can wear these while your things dry."

He helped John Thomas into the clothes— a white linen shirt and brown homespun trousers. There were shoes and stockings, too.

John Thomas went outside. Isabel was waiting.

"You look almost like my brother," she said. "Those are his clothes."

"Will he mind if I wear them?" asked John Thomas.

"He won't know it," she said. "He's away in Massachusetts. He's in school there. I'm Isabel Hunt," she told him, "but you know that already. Are you the older boy or the younger one?"

"I don't know what you mean," he said.

"You *are* one of the Simpson boys, aren't you?" she asked.

"No," he said.

"Oh!" she said. "Oh, my goodness!" She put her hands over her face.

"What's the matter?" he asked.

"There's a new family down the road," she said. "I heard there were two boys. I heard they were coming to call, and I thought you must be one of them." She asked, "Who *are* you?"

"I'm John Thomas," he said. "I'm from Half-Moon Valley." He told her about his bird and about how Tad Tripp had stolen it. "That's why I'm here," he said. "I'm looking for two men and a boy. Maybe you've seen them go by?"

"No, I haven't," she said, "but maybe someone else has. Come in, and I'll ask."

Chapter 7

Isabel's father had not seen the Tripp brothers. Neither had her mother.

John Thomas looked at the north road and the east road. He did not know which to take.

"Wait till your clothes dry," said Isabel. "Then you can make up your mind."

She showed him the house. There were rugs and curtains. There were pictures on the walls. There were chairs, chests, and tables made of dark, shining wood.

There was one room with shelves of books on every wall.

John Thomas looked into a book. "I could read this," he said. "It's about a king."

"It's a history book," said Isabel.

"Are there any about birds?" he asked.

"Oh, yes." She showed him a large book. On almost every page were pictures of birds. They looked at the pictures together. They came to one of a crow.

"Is this like your bird?" she asked.

"No," he said. "My bird is white."

"I hope you find it," she said.

"I have to find the Tripp brothers first," he said.

"I have an idea," said Isabel. "There's a dance tonight. You can come with us. A lot of people will be there, and you might hear something about those brothers."

"What is a dance?" he asked.

Isabel looked surprised. "Don't you really know?"

"No," he said.

"Well, there's music," she said, "and people dance."

"I don't know how to dance," John Thomas said.

"It doesn't matter," she said. "You can watch. Wouldn't you like to go?"

"Yes," he said.

The dance was being held in a long building on the bank of the river. It was a mill shed, Isabel told John Thomas. He followed her and her mother and father inside. The place was bright with lantern light. People stood about, talking and laughing. Some of them spoke to Isabel and her father and mother. John Thomas felt shy.

Then the dance began and he forgot to feel shy. Two men played fiddles. Another played a guitar. The sounds they made were like the wind and running water and birds singing. He said to himself, "This is music—I am hearing music!"

The dancers moved as if they were flying. Sometimes they danced in a circle. Sometimes they moved back and forth. Always they were in time with the music.

John Thomas and Isabel were sitting side by side. He asked her, "Do you know how to dance?"

"Oh, yes," she said.

"Could I learn?" he asked.

"Yes," she said. "It's easy. I could teach you."

A young man asked Isabel to dance.

"Thank you, Oliver," she said, "but I'm with John."

Oliver sat down by them.

Isabel said, "John is looking for his bird. It's a white crow."

"A *white* crow?" said Oliver.

"There aren't many in all the world," she said. "Three brothers came to John's house, and one of them took his bird."

"Three brothers?" said Oliver. "Two men and a boy?"

"Yes!" said John Thomas. "Did you see them?"

"No," said Oliver. "But my cousin did. They were at the Pickett place. They wanted to buy some land."

"Did the boy have my bird?" asked John Thomas.

"My cousin didn't say," said Oliver.

Later, as they walked home, Isabel told John Thomas how to get to the Pickett place. "Take the river trail. You'll know the house when you see it. It's made of brick."

Early the next morning, John Thomas was on his way. He was wearing his old clothes again.

He came to the brick house. He knocked. An old man opened the door.

John Thomas said, "I'm looking for the three Tripp brothers."

"They were here yesterday," said the man. "I don't know where they went."

A little girl looked out from behind him. "I think I saw them this morning," she said. "They were in the stump ground."

"Where is that?" asked John Thomas.

The girl pointed. "You go across the road and down that path."

John Thomas found the stump ground. It was a clearing where all the trees had been cut. Only the stumps were left.

He heard voices. He stopped and listened.

On the far side of the stump ground, a man came out of the woods. Behind him came another man and a boy. They were the Tripp brothers.

They saw John Thomas. They drew close together and stood there. He went toward them.

The two men, Len and Ernie, looked at him. The boy, Tad, looked down.

"What do you want?" asked Len.

"I want my bird," said John Thomas.

"We haven't got it," said Len.

"You took White Bird," John Thomas said to Tad.

"You gave it to him," said Len.

"No, I didn't," said John Thomas.

"He said you did," said Len. "Anyway, it was an ugly bird. It was a hard thing to carry. It got in the way."

"Where is it?" asked John Thomas.

"We let it go," said Len.

"But it couldn't fly," said John Thomas. "It couldn't take care of itself."

Tad spoke up. "It *could* fly—a little. It flew off—not very high, but it was flying."

Len walked away. Tad and Ernie followed him. But Tad came back. "Down the trail about a mile, just on the other side of the bridge—that's where I left the bird," he said. "They made me let it go. It was just yesterday. You might—you might still find it."

Then he ran across the stump ground after his brothers.

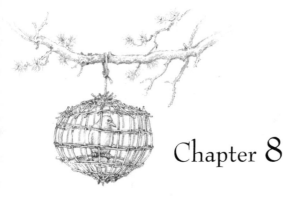

Chapter 8

John Thomas went back down the trail until he came to the bridge.

"White Bird!" he called.

He went into the woods. "Bird!" he called. "White Bird!"

At the edge of the woods, he came upon a little farm with a cabin, fields, and rail fences. A boy was sitting on one of the fences. His clothes were ragged. His face was thin and brown.

He looked at John Thomas a while before he spoke. "Do you live around here?"

"No," said John Thomas.

"What's your name?" asked the boy.

John Thomas told him.

"I'm Nim Timberlake," said the boy. "My father is Nim Timberlake, too. Did you come to see him?"

"No," said John Thomas. "I'm looking for my bird."

"Your what?" asked Nim.

"My bird. Somebody stole it and turned it loose somewhere around here," said John Thomas.

"What did it look like?" asked Nim.

"It's a white crow," said John Thomas. "It had a broken wing." He saw a strange look on Nim's face, and he said, "You saw it, didn't you?"

Nim slid down off the fence. "Yes," he said. "Yes, I did."

"Where?" asked John Thomas.

"Over there, by that rock," said Nim.

"Where did it go?" asked John Thomas.

"I went to the house and told the others to come and see," said Nim, "and—and—"

John Thomas waited.

"While I was in the house," said Nim, "there was a shot."

John Thomas stood still.

"My brother was out hunting," said Nim, "and he—"

John Thomas said, "He shot my bird."

"Yes," said Nim. "He never saw anything like it before, and he had to shoot it. John Thomas—"

"What?"

"I buried your bird," said Nim. "Do you want to know where?"

"No," said John Thomas.

"You can come up to the house if you want to," said Nim.

"I don't want to," said John Thomas.

"Well then, I've got a place in the woods," said Nim. "Nobody else knows about it. We can go there."

John Thomas went with him. Nim's place was a hollow in a thicket of bushes. It was like a room. They lay on the ground.

"I can see you're all tired out," said Nim. "You better rest a while before you go home."

"I'm not going home," said John Thomas.

"Don't you have to go back to your father and mother?" asked Nim.

"I don't have a father or mother," said John

Thomas. "I don't have anyone. There was Luke, but he let them take my bird."

"Who is Luke?" asked Nim.

John Thomas began to talk. He told about Luke and Half-Moon Valley. He told about the cradle that had come down the river. He told about White Bird.

After a while he didn't know whether Nim was listening or not, but he couldn't seem to stop. As he talked, he grew more and more tired. His eyes were closing. He could feel himself going to sleep.

In the morning, Nim brought John Thomas some bread and butter.

"I wish you could stay with us. I truly do," Nim said. "But my mother says there are too many of us already."

"I can probably find a place in town," said John Thomas.

He and Nim said good-bye.

John Thomas walked back to town. He stopped at Dave Cressey's store.

"I was just thinking about you," said Dave. "Did you have any luck finding your bird?"

"My bird is dead," said John Thomas.

Dave said, "I'm mighty sorry. You went to a lot of trouble to find it, too."

"Yes, I did," said John Thomas.

"Sit down," said Dave. "Rest your legs before you start home."

"I'm not going home," said John Thomas. "Couldn't I stay and help you in the store?"

"I'd like that," said Dave. "I'd like it fine. But the fact is, I've got all the help I need."

"Oh," said John Thomas.

"Anyway, it's best for you to go on home," said Dave. "Luke will be worrying about you."

"I don't care," said John Thomas. "He let them take my bird, and now I don't care."

"Wait a minute," said Dave. "He let them take your bird, and you don't like that. But aren't there any good things? Didn't I hear that he picked you up when you came down the river in a cradle? When you were little, didn't he feed you and take care of you?"

"He told me things that weren't so," said John Thomas. "All the things he told me about the world—they weren't so."

"Maybe they were to him," said Dave. "Maybe he sees the world one way and you see it another. You say you don't care and you're not going home, but where *will* you go? Someday you can make your own way, but you're not ready yet."

A woman came in. Dave sold her a ball of string. When she was gone, he went back to John Thomas.

"If you want to stay tonight, you can," said Dave. "But if you start now, you can get home before dark."

"I'll start now," said John Thomas.

First the trail out of town. Then the steep hill path. Then the narrower path that led down into the valley.

Evening had come. The cabin was in shadow. John Thomas went up to it. He was not sure he wanted to go in.

The door opened and Luke came out.

"So, you came back," he said.

John Thomas said nothing.

"Where did you go?" asked Luke.

"To town," answered John Thomas. "To find the Tripp brothers."

"You didn't find them, did you?" said Luke.

"Yes, I did," said John Thomas. "My bird is dead."

"You're a sorry sight," said Luke. "All dirty and raggedy and your hair in your eyes."

John Thomas pushed back his hair. He turned and went down to the river. He washed his face and hands.

A bird flew out of the willows. It looked white against the sky. He thought of White Bird and was sad.

But when he thought of White Bird, he remembered Dave Cressey and the store. He remembered Isabel—and the dancing—and the music. He remembered Nim. . . .

He heard footsteps. Luke had come down to the river.

"So, you had to go out in the world," said Luke. "You had to go find out how it was. You found out it was the way I said, didn't you? . . . Didn't you?"

"No," said John Thomas. "And I'm going again."

Luke said, "You'll never get over that bird, will you? You'll always blame me."

John Thomas was listening to the river. It was like a quiet voice.

Luke said, "I did the best I could, and you're getting ready to leave—like everybody else."

He sounded tired. He looked lonely standing there. John Thomas thought of him alone in the cabin, alone in the valley. What was it Dave Cressey had said? ". . . He picked you up when you came down the river in a cradle. . . ." Luke must have been a young man then. He wasn't young now.

John Thomas said, "I'm not going yet."

Luke was on his way up to the cabin. John Thomas started after him. He said again, "I'm not going yet. And when I do, maybe—maybe you can go, too. Luke, didn't you hear me?"

"I heard you." Luke stopped. He stood there in the path and waited for John Thomas.

About the Author

CLYDE ROBERT BULLA is an outstanding children's book author, with more than sixty books and many awards to his credit. About *White Bird* he writes, "At the time I started this story, I took a vacation trip to Greece. There I saw a boy who looked the way I had always pictured John Thomas. He was standing on a pier, looking out to sea. Near him was a white bird, probably a sea gull. I realized they belonged together, and the story became *White Bird.*"

Clyde Robert Bulla grew up in King City, Missouri, and now lives in Los Angeles.

About the Illustrator

DONALD COOK has been drawing and painting for as long as he can remember. He turned to book illustration only recently, and now says that "children's book illustration is the most satisfying work I do." In addition, he teaches art to children in upstate New York, where he lives with his wife and child.